ALMOST
BIG
ENOUGH

written and illustrated
by
Jean Tamburine

ABINGDON PRESS

NASHVILLE
NEW YORK

For boys and girls who are
almost big enough and for
those who are big enough
for school

And especially
for my Lisa and Robbie

ALMOST BIG ENOUGH

Susy was sad. Susy was lonesome. Everyone she knew had gone to school. Her brother Bob had gone away on the school bus. The children who lived across the street had gone away on the school bus.

But not Susy. Susy was too little to go to school. Every day it was the same. All the children went away on the school bus. But Susy was left behind.

"Will I be big enough tomorrow?" Susy asked her mother.

"Not tomorrow," said Mother, "but in a little while."

"A little while? How long is that?" Susy asked.

"A few days, a few nights—after your birthday. Why don't you play in the yard?" Mother asked.

Susy scuffed her feet and bowed her head. She thought she was going to cry.

She ran to her secret place under the china-
berry tree. The soft grass felt cool against
her face. Her duck and her hen and her
cat were sorry Susy was so lonesome.

"Quack!" said the duck.

"Cluck, cluck," said the hen.

"Meow, Meow, Meow!" said the cat.

Susy lifted her head. "One quack, two
clucks, and three meows—you can count!
I'll play school with you."

The duck and the hen and the cat stayed
very still—well, almost still—while Susy
brought crayons, paper, scissors, glue,
chalk, a slate, and an eraser. And that's not
all. She brought a tin horn, a tambourine,

a drum, a whistle, four paper party hats, and a box of chocolate cookies for lunch.

She sat on a tree stump and pretended to read to the duck, the hen, and the cat.

"Do you like that story?" Susy asked.

"Quack," said the duck.

"Cluck, cluck," said the hen.

"Meow, Meow, Meow!" said the cat.

Susy looked at them, and a big tear splashed down her cheek. She said, "I'll tell you a bothersome secret. I really can't read."

The duck and the hen and the cat just looked at poor Susy.

"I'll tell you another secret," said Susy, "I really don't know what they do in school."

The duck and the hen and the cat started to move away.

"Don't go," Susy cried, "I don't know what they do in school, but there's a lady they call the teacher, and she tells everybody what to do." The duck and the hen and the cat said nothing. Not a word. Not a sound.

Susy clapped her hands. "I have an idea.
I'll be the teacher. I'll tell you what to do.
Watch me. You must do what I do."

Susy ran very fast. The duck and the
hen and the cat ran too. Susy rolled on
the grass. The duck and the hen and the
cat rolled on the grass.

Susy said, "Let's see who can scream the loudest."

"Quack," said the duck.

"Cluck, cluck," said the hen.

"Meow, meow, MEOW-W-W!" said the cat.

"Louder, louder!" shouted Susy. Two frightened birds flew right out of their nest in the tree.

Susy's mother came to the back door. "What's all the noise?" she asked.

"We're playing school," Susy answered, "and I'm the teacher."

"They are not quite so noisy in school," Mother said, "and the teachers don't shout."

"What do they do in school?" Susy asked.

"They sing and march and draw pictures and paste ..."

"We'll sing," Susy called to the duck and the hen and the cat. She began to sing:

A B C D E F G

H I J K L M N O P

Q R S T U V

W and X Y Z

NOW I'VE LEARNED MY ABC

AND I'M HAPPY AS CAN BE.

"Quack," said the duck.

"Cluck, cluck," said the hen.

"Meow, meow, meow-w-w!" said the cat.

"Susy!" Mother called. "Not so loud."

"I guess we'll have to whisper," Susy said to the duck and the hen and the cat, "but let's see who can jump the highest."

The duck was too fat. She just fell, PLOP.

The hen had short legs. She just fell, PLUNK.

But the cat could jump. High.

Susy jumped up and down, but the cat jumped higher.

"You're the best jumper," Susy said and patted the cat on the head.

"But don't you be sad," she said to the duck and the hen, "if you can't jump you can do something else."

"I know," Susy said, "we'll wear funny hats and make silly faces."

"Quack," said the duck, looking very silly in his pointed hat.

"Cluck, cluck," said the hen, whose hat was much too big.

"Meow, meow, meow-w-w!" said the cat, who kept his nose in the air so he could see out from under his hat.

The duck grew tired and sat down, PLOP!

The hen bumped into the duck, and fell down, PLUNK!

The cat fell over the two of them.

"I guess you're not old enough to go to school either," Susy scolded, "but I'm tired too. Let's take a nap."

Susy lay down on the grass. The duck and the hen and the cat lay down. Soon they were all fast asleep.

Susy was still asleep when Bob came home on the school bus.

"I have a surprise for you," he called to Susy.

"What is it?" Susy asked, rubbing her eyes.

"Mother said I couldn't tell you until supper," Bob said.

"Is it gumdrop candy?" Susy wanted to know right away.

"No, but I mustn't tell what it is."

"Is it a toy?"

"I can't tell you, Susy, until we have our supper," said Bob, and he ran away to play.

Susy thought suppertime would never come. The duck and the hen and the cat wanted to play, but Susy said, "Please go away. I'm very busy—waiting."

When Father came home, Mother called, "Susy! Bob! It's suppertime."

Susy ran into the house. She washed her hands without being told and sat quietly at her place. Father, Mother, and Bob sat down. It was Susy's turn to say the prayer before meals. She was so busy waiting to hear Bob's secret she forgot about the prayer.

"Please say the prayer, Susy," Mother said.

"We thank you, God, in every way, for all you give to us this day. Amen," said Susy, "and, now, what's the secret, Bob?"

"My teacher said you may visit kindergarten tomorrow."

"You mean I'm not too little?" Susy asked.

"Not too little to visit," said Bob. "Mother will take you."

Oh, Susy was so excited. She tried to go to sleep quickly that night, but as she lay in bed she kept humming to herself, "I'm going to school. I'm going to school. I'm almost big enough. I'm going to school."

The next morning Susy helped Mother choose her dress and shoes and socks to wear to school.

She had a very special feeling as if it were Christmas or her birthday. And she could hardly believe it when after a short drive in the car Mother said, "Here's the school, Susy."

Susy was glad Mother was with her.
School was a very big place.

They walked down a hall with many doors.

They stopped before a door with a sign
that read

KINDERGARTEN

"Open the door, Susy," said Mother.

Susy was frightened. What was behind such a big closed door?

She turned the knob and peeked inside.

Kindergarten

Tambourine

Susy saw rows and rows of boys and
girls. This was school. A tall lady came
toward Susy.

"This is Miss Jones, the teacher," Mother
said to Susy. Susy hid behind Mother and
peeked at Miss Jones. Miss Jones had a

nice friendly smile. She looked a little bit like Mother.

"Hello, Susy," said Miss Jones.

"Hello," whispered Susy.

"Come, Susy," said Miss Jones as Mother waved goodbye.

"This is where we hang our hats and coats."

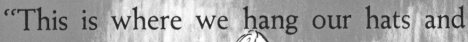

Susy felt as if she would burst with happiness. Miss Jones said, "We must see if everyone is here today. Will each of you say your name, please?"

Susy sat quietly while all the boys and girls said their names. Then each one said, "Good morning, Miss Jones."

Three of the children were asked to be helpers. Susy wondered what that meant until she remembered that when she put her toys away or dried the dishes she was Mother's helper.

These three children were going to help
Miss Jones. One of them held the flag
while all the children said together:

"I pledge allegiance to the flag of the
United States of America, and to the Re-
public for which it stands, one Nation
under God, indivisible, with liberty and
justice for all."

The other two helpers straightened
chairs, picked up crayons, and carried
messages to other rooms for Miss Jones.
Miss Jones said, "Boys and girls, you may
do whatever you wish until I sound a

chord on the piano." Some boys and girls
played in a two-story playhouse. Some
modeled with clay. Some worked with
scissors, paper, and glue. Others built with
blocks or put on smocks and painted pictures.

Susy was so excited she wanted to try everything.

"Susy, come see the turtles," Miss Jones called to her. Susy peered into the glass aquarium, and there on the other side peering back were two big brown eyes.

"Oh, what big eyes you have, turtle," Susy said, and then she laughed. The big brown eyes didn't belong to a turtle but to a little boy who was looking through the other side of the aquarium.

His name was Stevie.

It was a very busy morning for Susy. First she thought she liked best the time when Miss Jones turned on the record player. The boys and girls skipped and danced. Susy danced too.

She was ready to rest when Miss Jones called, "Nap time!"

At nap time each child had a little rug to lie on. Miss Jones gave a rug to Susy.

Susy decided lunchtime was really best of all. There were cookies and milk for everyone. As they ate, Miss Jones read a story.

Susy had never done so many different things in one morning. But she was glad to see Mother standing in the doorway when Miss Jones said, "It is time to go home, boys and girls. Put everything away and put on your coats and hats."

Susy was very happy. Her eyes were shining.

"Thank you for such a nice time," she said.

Susy put her hand in Mother's.

"Oh, I've had such a good time."

"I know you did, dear," said Mother, "but the duck and the hen and the cat have missed you."

"Let's go home," said Susy. "I have something very important to tell them."

The duck and the hen and the cat were waiting in the backyard.

"Do you know what?" she cried. "School is even more fun than the way we played."

"Quack," said the duck.

"Cluck, cluck," said the hen.

"Meow, meow, meow-w-w," said the cat.

"Yes, I know," Susy laughed. "I'm almost big enough."